ROYAL TROUBLE the MYSTERIOUS SEA

The Mysterious Sea (Royal Trouble #2)

Text Copyright © 2019 by Hope Erica Schultz
Illustrations by Jeff Crosby.

For more information, write:
CBAY Books
PO Box 670296
Dallas, TX 75367

Children's Brains are Yummy Books
Dallas, Texas
www.cbaybooks.blog

Paperback ISBN: 978-1-944821-44-9
ebook ISBN: 978-1-944821-45-6

For CPSIA information, please see:
cbaybooks.blog/cpsia-information/

Printed in the United States of America.

*For Ciaran S, who has all the brilliance
with far fewer explosions*

Zap stood on its stubby legs and took a step closer along Donal's work table. "Five more minutes elapsed. Commencing shock in ten ... nine ... eight ..."

Donal was busy with his latest project. He didn't even glance at Zap. He tightened two wires together, then hooked a spring over both of them. "Nearly there ..."

Zap was not programmed to respond to that. Two more small steps, and a blue spark came from the little android's hand.

"Yow!" Donal grabbed a set of tiny plyers to twist the wires and spring into place ... and the room's gaslights went out. He finished the maneuver in the darkness, then stood up with a sigh. "Who programmed you to turn out the lights?" Donal paused a moment as the lights flickered back on, then looked at Zap. The clock that made up the android's middle was at quarter to two. "Right. I did. Party today."

The mirror on the wall showed a smudge of soot on his nose, and his blond hair was a little on end from the electric shock, but all in all, Donal thought he looked presentable. He rubbed at his nose with his sleeve and, when Zap raised its right hand again, reluctantly turned away from his latest project.

Someone knocked on the door as he approached it, and he opened it up to find his mother. Queen Melia was holding a box out, a strange expression on her face.

"What's wrong?"

"Nothing's wrong," she said. Her smile looked a little crooked. "I just wanted to bring you something before the party." She handed him the box.

"Zap, sleep," Donal said absently as he put the box on the table. His mother was twisting the edge of her sleeve.

"Before you were born ... your father and I

talked. He was an adventurer, and he knew he wasn't cut out to be a good father, and he didn't want to be a bad one. So, he left. This is one of the things he left behind. He said it was for someone who wanted to go places but also wanted to be able to find their way back."

My father. It didn't sound right, not like *my mother*, or *my friends*, or *my uncle* all did. Donal opened the box carefully. Inside was an intricate brass device with a spyglass attached, two mirrors, and a sweeping bottom edge marked in tiny lines.

"It's a sextant, for measuring latitude," his mother offered.

Donal nodded. Latitude was how far something was from the equator and on which side. "What about longitude, how far around the world you've gone?"

His mother smiled and gestured at Zap. "For that, you just need a clock, set for true noon where you're starting, and measured against true noon where you end up."

Donal held the sextant carefully. "I can't wait to figure it out."

There was a distant thudding of the front door

knockers, and Donal frowned. He shrugged and set the sextant down. "After the party."

There were not a lot of other kids that Donal hung out with at home. Kids his age didn't tend to be ready for the kind of inventing he did, and their parents complained about the explosions. Besides, he lost track of what he was doing and where he was supposed to be when he was in his workshop.

The kids from the other three Waveborn islands were different. For one thing, they were all royalty, too. Mom and her friends had fought pirates, and Mom had been the one to figure out how to raise the islands from the bottom of the sea. She had ended up ruler of West Waveborn.

Then, the four kids had all had a massive adventure in the spring when their parents had been kidnapped and replaced with android Regents, bringing them all closer together. After that, they all knew they could count on each other, no matter what.

The first through the door were Jes and her parents, King Willem and Queen Eris of East Waveborn, with Jes's big sister Alex right behind them. Jes was wearing a fancy blue dress, but with her boots peeking out underneath. She handed Donal a present as she came in. "It's new goggles with lenses to slide up and down depending on the light."

"Jes!" Queen Eris reproved.

Jes winced. "Sorry! I've just been thinking about it the whole while here. It was a four-hour trip because Daddy didn't want to fly."

Given what had happened the last time King Willem had been in an airship, Donal thought that was understandable. "Thank you," he said out loud.

Amalia and her parents, King Phineas and Queen Anya from North Waveborn were next. Amalia was also wearing a dress, but with a sword. She shoved a present into his hands. "I was going to get you a sword, but I remembered that you don't like them, so I got you goggles that you can adjust to see tiny things or things far away."

Donal's mother looked like she was trying not to laugh, and the other adults were looking at the ceiling. Donal smiled. "Thank you, they sound great."

Chris ran in well ahead of his parents, King

Darby and Queen Lily of South Waveborn. "Donal! You gotta open this! It's a pair of goggles with *night vision*!"

The adults were laughing out loud now. Donal ignored them. "That's so cool! Now I have goggles for EVERYTHING!"

Jes nodded. "You can't have too many of your favorite things. Like books."

"Swords!" Amalia cheered.

"Implements of destruction!" Chris's stomach chose that moment to growl. "And food!"

Donal's mother laughed. "Well, we have food. Come along in."

Uncle Kegan joined them in the Dining Room, clutching a package wrapped in brown paper and twine. He moved like a bird, quick and nervous. Looking at him, Donal always felt like he was looking at himself in a mirror, but older.

Presents were pushed off for food—meat pies and soups, but mostly food the way Donal liked it, one thing by itself, nothing mixed together. Chicken, vegetables, and potatoes were better when you could tell what they were. There were also fancier foods for the grown-ups, Alex, and Chris. Chris, Amalia had once pointed out, would eat anything that didn't try to eat him first.

Even Chris was winding down when Kegan slid the package over to Donal. "Happy Birthday."

"Kegan, you're worse than the children," Donal's mother scolded.

"It's better to allow some time to digest before dessert," Kegan answered. "I'm the oldest one here, so I get to go first."

Donal ignored the argument as he examined the package. It was shaped like a length of pipe, about the size of his forearm, but it was surprisingly light. He carefully untied the string and peeled back the paper.

Inside was a rolled piece of leather with drawings on it. Words in a language he didn't recognize were interspersed with numbers he did. Longitude and latitude, and a curved mark almost like an X.

"It's a map," he said. It was hard not to jump up from the table and go study it immediately.

"A treasure map?" Chris asked.

"Possibly," Uncle Kegan said. "That language is a little like ancient Dorish, but I'm only guessing at what it says. It's much older than it should be, for how well preserved it is. Leather usually only lasts a century or two."

Donal did calculations in his head. "It's not that far from here. A week by ship, but only a day or two with the skiff."

King Willem looked slightly green. "That's the little submersible airship that looks like a giant bubble?"

Amalia dashed over to see, with Jes and Chris close behind. "Summer break is just starting! The four of us can pack supplies and go exploring, just like old times!"

King Phineas cleared his throat. "No," he said.

Amalia turned to him. "But Daddy ..."

"It's not really appropriate to send four nine and ten-year-old kids out alone like that," her mother, Queen Anya, said.

Alex stood up suddenly. "Are we all going to pretend that last Spring never happened? These are the same kids who outsmarted five androids and a pirate, saved King Gregor, and kept the Waveborn islands from being sunk back into the sea. Now you're worried about a camping trip?"

Donal's mother stood up too, but she was smiling. "They are the same people who did that. They were brave and capable and managed it all on their own—but they shouldn't have had to. Let them be children a little longer. Let there be someone to help them."

"Maybe Alex could—" Queen Eris suggested.

Alex made a chopping motion with her hands. "I can't. I have to study for the entrance exams at the University."

Donal was not sure if he was disappointed or not. Alex could be great, but she and Jes fought if they were cooped up together for very long.

"Uncle Kegan?" he asked. It was the most logical choice.

"I'm afraid I'm prone to sea sickness. And air sickness. And time away from my lab sickness." Kegan smiled. "But I can't wait to hear all about it."

If we even get to go, Donal thought glumly.

Jes spoke up from beside him. "If Mrs. Clemens would agree, we should bring her."

All the adults seemed to take a breath and let it out with sounds of agreement.

"Who?" Chris asked.

"Our housekeeper," Jes explained.

Amalia and Chris opened their mouths, and Jes made a jabbing motion with her hand. "Trust me," she hissed.

Donal considered having a housekeeper along. He wasn't even sure who their current housekeeper was; the last one had quit just a few weeks ago after a day of more than typical explosions. None of the ones he could remember would have been of any use. Still, all that mattered was going.

It was only after dessert that Jes found a moment to whisper her explanation. "She'll be perfect. She was a navigator under Dark Mathis."

"Your housekeeper is a pirate?" Donal asked.

Jes nodded enthusiastically.

Donal smiled. "Do you think they'll let us leave tomorrow?"

Packing for an expedition did not, it turned out, happen in one night, or even in one day. They needed water and food that wouldn't go bad too quickly. There were plans and contingency plans. Amalia insisted on bringing materials to make booby traps, several coils of rope, and a second sword in case something happened to her first. Jes kept a list of everything anyone mentioned, and it just got longer and longer. And in the meantime, Donal had to add a fifth seat to the skiff and go over every piece of equipment on board.

On the sixth day, they were gathered in Donal's library, around a huge wooden table, going over final details. It was starting to get dark, and they had turned on the gaslights. A fire warmed the evening chill, and the room felt cozy. It was also beginning to feel like a cage. It was great that the adults were leaving them alone to prepare ... but did there have to be quite so much to do? Were they ever going to get to leave?

"This book says that the most dangerous thing on a ship is fire. What do we do about that?" Jes asked.

"Can't we just let in some water?" Chris objected, juggling three candlesticks. "I know this is important, but isn't there ever an *end* to the planning?

Jes hauled over two huge books and dumped them on the table in front of him. "Fine. Every time you drop a candlestick, or whatever you're playing with, try to look up one of the words on the map in these. That will keep you out of trouble."

"Hah! As if I'm going to drop—" Chris fumbled a candlestick and turned to the books with a sigh. "Right. On it."

Jes turned back to Donal. "Fire. Without drowning, preferably."

Donal smiled. "That, I have an answer for."

From the half dozen pouches hanging from

his belt, he pulled out the green one. "Alchemical fire extinguisher. Never leave home without it. It's the only substance that will stop alchemical fire quickly, and it works just as well on regular fire." He shook a single, marble-sized, black pellet out of the pouch and into his hand. "Go ahead, throw it on the fire."

Jes looked at him dubiously. Amalia stepped up and picked up the pellet. "That's a pretty big fire," she said, gesturing at the fireplace.

"No, a house fire is a pretty big fire, and you'd need more than one of these to put out that. This is an ordinary fire. One will work on a bonfire, usually."

Amalia shrugged and tossed it in. The fire flared up, incredibly bright, and then went out.

Chris looked up from the dictionaries. "I'd like twenty for my birthday, please!"

They all laughed. A knock on the door stopped them, and then a footman peeked in cautiously. "Mrs. Clemens is here to see you, Prince Donal."

Mrs. Clemens looked like somebody's grand-mother. She was only a little taller than Donal was, with a round face and graying hair. She handed him several sheets of parchment when he greeted her, and she didn't smile.

"What are these—" Donal began, looking at the sheets. There were four, all in different handwriting.

"Letters of reference, Captain Donal. I wouldn't expect you to hire me without some proof of what I can do." She tilted her head slightly. "Do you prefer your title instead?"

Donal blinked a little. "You can just call me Donal."

Mrs. Clemens shook her head. "On land, if you like, but not aboard ship. I need to remember that you're the one calling the shots and calling you Captain is the fastest way to do that." She pointed to the parchment. "And speaking of shots, you'll see that I'm capable with black powder, cannon, beam weapons, cutlasses, and frying pans."

Donal blinked again. "Frying pans?"

"That was to see if you were paying attention. I can navigate, provision, cook, repair less complex machinery, and follow orders. I don't know how to pilot either an airship or a submersible, but I can learn if you'd like to teach me."

Donal felt like his eyes had to be crossing, but

14

Mrs. Clemens, housekeeper and pirate, seemed to be content to wait for an answer. He glanced again at the references. "Thank you, I think you'll do."

"Thank you, Captain. I'll see to stowing the supplies then if that meets with your approval. Did you want to leave in the morning?"

I want to leave right now. It had taken almost a week to fit a fifth seat into the skiff and update all the equipment. Still it was evening, and by the time the supplies were packed, it would be night. A good night's sleep was probably smart.

"First thing in the morning," he confirmed and went to tell the others the good news.

Jes and Amalia were now gathered around the copy of the map that Donal had made while Chris still had the two dictionaries in old languages.

"The closest word in old Dornish is *vallere*, a verb meaning to ignite. In ancient Kesch, it's *voler*, which means light." Chris looked up, his short knots of hair bobbing.

"Light and fire and sight all have overlap, so I'm betting it's a word with one of those meanings," Jes said.

"Still it would be nice to know if it means

we'll see something or be set on fire by it," Amalia pointed out.

Donal cleared his throat. Everyone looked up, and he raised his hands in victory. "We leave in the morning!"

Amalia and Chris cheered while Jes looked at the map. "We're going to have to bring the dictionaries with us."

"Bring them," Donal agreed. "We may find clues once we get there."

"We may find treasure!" Chris crowed.

Amalia laughed, and Jes shook her head. "What would you even do with treasure?"

"Brag about finding it. A lot."

Chris put his dark hand down on the map, and Amalia put her brown one on top of it. Jes's pale hand was next, and then Donal put his tanned hand on top, sealing the bargain. "To adventure," Donal said, "with or without treasure."

Donal realized by the time the others were down to breakfast that he might as well have forgotten about the good night's sleep. Chris had talked to him until Donal had to sic Zap on him and then had apparently gone off to talk to the girls until crazy late. Chris was as chipper as ever, but Amalia and Jes were bleary eyed. Amalia asked for coffee, adding in about half a cup of sugar, and after a few minutes, Jes did the same.

"I wonder how we would go about doing tests on Chris's metabolism?" Donal mused. "Does he eat so much because he simply never sleeps?"

"If we starve him, will he let *us* sleep?" Amalia asked. She held out her mug blindly for a refill of coffee, and Donal's mom filled it.

"He'll be quiet tonight," Jes promised. "Mrs. Clemens packed her *wooden spoon.*"

After the letters about her skill with cutlasses and firearms, a wooden spoon seemed tame. Still, Chris settled down to his usual four course breakfast. Donal caught his mother's eye at the other end of the table and smiled.

"We'll see how far the communications work," he said. "We'll have to be back in a week for more supplies, even if we haven't found anything yet."

"I know you'll be fine," his mother said calmly although she was twisting her sleeve again. "And I hope it will be a good break for all of you."

Amalia muttered about breaking *Chris*, and the moment was over.

The skiff did look like a bubble with brass fins. Mrs. Clemens had stored supplies under the floor, under the seats, and around her own seat in the back. There was barely room to walk in the craft, and Jes had to duck her head a little when she did. She had grown from the spring, and she was the tallest of the five.

Jes had also brought the dictionaries as she had threatened. She settled back into her seat with them while Amalia and Chris argued about who would sit up front with Donal.

"I think Mrs. Clemens had better be first," Donal decided. "Everyone else has a basic idea of how to fly the skiff, so it's her turn."

Amalia pouted but didn't object while Chris grabbed the back chair by the food. He was reaching out a hand when Mrs. Clemens spoke up from the front. "If food is missing, Your Highness, I'm taking it out of your lunch ration."

"She didn't even turn around!" Amalia hissed.

"I told you she was great," Jes replied.

Chris had both hands back inside his chair, so Donal turned his attention to Mrs. Clemens. She grinned at him and gestured to the controls.

"Ready when you are, Captain."

"That tunnel to the left leads under water, and we could take off there if we didn't want to be seen. This way is prettier, though." Donal pushed the throttle slowly open and eased the skiff through the tunnel straight ahead. They came out through an opening in the cliff below the castle, with the rest of West Waveborn spread below them like a collection of children's toys surrounded by ocean.

Take off was easy with no one shooting at them, and Donal honestly preferred it that way. The sun was bright, the sky was clear, and the sea beneath them was a thousand shades of blue. The skiff rose quickly in the sky, hovered like a bumble bee, and then picked up speed as Donal turned them west.

By sunset, each of them had taken a turn flying the skiff. They were still, barely, able to communicate with Donal's mother and had sent word that all was still well. The person on lookout used Donal's new distance goggles to see further.

19

They saw a few ships, one airship headed towards the south, and a pod of dolphins on their way. Sea birds were common at first, but soon there were none. West of the Waveborn islands, there weren't any land masses or islands on their maps for a long distance. The sea looked vast, and a little lonely.

Jes had deciphered two more words on the map, although they were still guesses. "*Su* appears to be a preposition and might mean in or under. I think *tace* is a noun, but related to height, falling, or climbing."

Amalia threw up her hands. "So, it might mean that we're going to fall into a fire or look up at a light."

"Or a hundred other things," Jes agreed. "That's what makes it fun!"

"How far into the night are you planning on flying?" Mrs. Clemens asked.

"If the night stays clear, all of it," Donal said. "If I slow our speed a little, we should be right on target at about true noon and can check by the clock. If it clouds over, it's safer to go underwater to travel, and that's slower."

Mrs. Clemens nodded. She didn't make any

comment, but Donal felt that her nod meant approval. "What order did you want us to sleep in?"

Jes and Amalia both yawned, and Donal grinned. "Why don't Chris and I stay awake for now, and we'll wake the rest of you as I need you."

The chairs reclined—another improvement—and Donal dimmed the interior lights to make it easier to fly by starlight. Within minutes everything was quiet.

"So, about the treasure," Chris stage-whispered.

"Chris," Donal said very, very softly, "if you mess up anybody's sleep tonight, you're going to walk the plank."

Mrs. Clemens took second watch, and Amalia and Jes took third. Sunlight was pouring in through the glass when Donal awoke the next morning. It was approaching noon when Jes pointed to a dim outline of a mountain coming up from the ocean. Smoke wafted up from it.

"I think I know what those words meant now," Jes said as they approached the volcano. "Fire mountain." Lava bubbled down inside the caldera.

"Let's hope *su* means under and not in."

21

The communications did not reach as far as the island. Donal confirmed their location at true noon and then took them underwater. There was no beach to land on, only the volcano's peak rising from the waves.

"At the very least, we get to map an active volcano," Donal reassured the others.

Chris sighed melodramatically. "How can you think about *science* when there's a chance at *treasure*?"

Donal shook his head, trying to imagine why anyone would prefer gold or jewels to discovering something new. Mrs. Clemens, at least, had her priorities straight. She offered to map the structures around the volcano as he piloted.

The falling lava, mixed with earlier lava tubes, had produced rock walls almost like lace. Small indentations held schools of fish, and there were tunnels that looked big enough to take the skiff into them.

A shark almost the size of the skiff swam by them, causing Amalia to grab her sword convulsively. "That's a whale shark," Donal reassured her. "They eat things too small to notice. Their mouths don't open enough to hurt us."

"What about that?" Chris asked. Just beyond the lights of the skiff, something bigger than a large ship stirred in the dark.

Donal cut the lights. The natural lights of some of the creatures—*bioluminescence*—lit the scene eerily. They could make out a snake like body, a head the size of the skiff, four limbs that were almost fins.

"Oh, that is a beauty," Mrs. Clemens breathed. "That could take down a whole ship of the line if the crew were stupid enough to turn their sixty-four cannons on it and make it mad."

That was not exactly reassuring, but Donal already

knew that not making it mad was key. They slowed down to a stop, closer than he would have liked.

"Are those eggs?" Jes asked. "It's a mother sea monster!"

The great head nuzzled eggs a little larger than cannon balls, and one baby emerged and uncurled. It was maybe three feet long, tiny next to its parent.

"Father," Donal said absently. "In sea monsters, the mother lays the eggs and leaves, and the father raises them."

They watched as egg after egg hatched, then Jes gasped. "The whale shark! Are the babies small enough for him to eat them?"

"No," Donal said. "And nothing will get past an adult sea monster. I'd worry for the whale shark, not about him."

"Too late," Chris said cheerfully.

They watched as the whale shark wandered close. The sea monster's neck snaked out, and in another moment, the babies were eating pieces of shark meat.

They stayed quiet while the babies fed and then were rounded up by their father and ushered away. Donal shook himself slightly, remembering.

"These are very few good examples of sea monster shells. Let's try to grab some."

They inched closer and then put on the exterior lights. Donal sent out an external arm to collect shards.

"That one didn't hatch," Jes pointed out. Sure enough, one luminous egg was still whole on the sea floor.

"That would be an amazing sample," Donal said. He maneuvered the arm closer, brushing against the shell.

The shell dimpled slightly, then burst open. A dark blue sea monster baby spilled out, blinking at them through huge green eyes.

At first, everyone except Donal had seemed paralyzed, just staring at the baby. Even when Donal had grabbed meat from Mrs. Clemen's stores, then maneuvered it out to the baby, everyone had stayed still and silent. Now, Donal was talking to it gently through the external speakers. The baby, in turn, was rubbing up against the skiff and crooning.

Jess shook herself, as though she'd been falling

asleep. "How will it survive without a parent?"

"Maybe we could lead it to its family, not get eaten ourselves, and sneak away?" Amalia offered. "It works with baby birds."

Chris made a rude noise. "I'd bet the parent birds weren't trying to eat you, though."

"We don't look like food," Donal said. He almost looked at Mrs. Clemens. She'd probably have an answer, but then he'd feel like this was her mission, not his. "I like Amalia's idea. We can spare four days before we have to head home for more supplies, and it's worth a try."

He called to Blot—the baby's color was like an inkblot, and it seemed as good a name as any—and headed in the direction the sea monster had gone. Blot followed along.

"Mrs. Clemens, do you want to try to catch a fish or two for Blot with the robot arm?"

"Aye, aye, Captain."

"Everybody else, look for sea monster signs." Donal sighed. He'd never had a pet—explosions and fur didn't mix—but he was starting to understand why people got so stubborn about them. He couldn't leave a small being that needed

27

him. Some responsibilities were too important to abandon.

Donal's voice was getting hoarse, and they still hadn't caught sight of the sea monster and the other hatchlings. Blot ignored any voice that wasn't Donal's, although it seemed happy enough with the fish Mrs. Clemens caught.

"There's a bunch of fish all schooling that way," Jes pointed to the right. "Should we look to see what they're running from?"

Amelia gripped her sword again but murmured her agreement. Donal nodded, keeping the skiff between Blot and the possible threat. There were plenty of things down here that would eat a baby sea monster if they got the chance. *What on this skiff could be used as a weapon?*

There was a shadow ahead, a hammerhead shark, but it was following the school of fish without any effort to catch them. *It's running, too.*

"Hold on," Donal called, then crooned to Blot to keep him close. There was a rock formation to their left, and beyond that was whatever the fish were trying to escape. Donal killed the lights and eased back on the power so that they were drifting as they turned around the rocks.

He slipped on the night vision goggles from Chris. Spots of bioluminescence in the darkness became a twilight scene with dozens of moving creatures that looked like Blot. "Hey, I think we've found them!"

The skiff shook suddenly, and the view port went dark except for some stalactite-looking masses on either side. "Um … the dad has found us?" Amalia suggested. "I thought you said we didn't look like food!"

"We don't." Donal flipped up the goggles and turned back on the lights. The full-grown sea monster had them gripped in his mouth but, fortunately, wasn't big enough to swallow them. Donal noted that the inside of the creature's mouth was violet rather than red, but the giant teeth were white; it had been too dark to notice what color the outside was.

The others were quiet although Donal saw that even Mrs. Clemens was holding on with white knuckles. He took a deep breath, discarding idea after idea. The safest thing was to act like a rock and wait for the monster to lose interest.

There was a worried sound from Blot, and

Donal gave a reassuring croon on the external speaker. Outside of the skiff was a small thud, and then the giant mouth released them. The skiff's lights shone on Blot, who was being nuzzled by the giant head—purple against Blot's indigo.

Donal held his breath as the other babies came up to their missing sibling and tasted the water around him with their tongues. They ranged in color from green to their father's purple, but the few others Blot's shade had purple eyes, not green. Maybe they recognized Blot as family, or maybe they were just getting to know him, but Blot seemed accepted.

Donal felt a little pang as he cut the lights again and set the skiff to slowly back out, away from the family of sea monsters. Blot didn't turn around, and Donal didn't want to distract the baby with any farewell. He pushed the goggles down to get a good look at the dark blue shape, and then he forced his attention back to the skiff.

They went slowly through the darkness for several minutes, no one talking, until Donal put the lights back on. "That was successful," he said. His voice sounded flat to him, and he remembered to smile. "Everyone okay?"

"That was awesome!" Chris exclaimed. "Only the skiff needs some kind of weapons."

Chris and Amalia got into a heated discussion on the best way to arm an airship that was also a submarine while Jes soon turned back to her dictionaries. Donal started a little at a touch on his shoulder.

"Would you like to find a secure spot to stop for the night?" Mrs. Clemens asked gently. "We've got three more days to search, and I suspect we'll all do better after a full night's sleep."

It was the closest she'd come to anything like taking charge. Donal knew that if he said no, she wouldn't argue, but he *was* tired. Probably they all were. He found a tunnel empty of apparent threats and set the skiff down. A few dials and switches, and the external alarms were set to wake them if anything troubled them.

Chris and the girls were talkative during supper, but Donal was silent. Mrs. Clemens was quiet, too. Once their eyes met, and she nodded slightly, as though she understood what he was feeling.

It would have been nice if *he* knew what he was feeling.

31

A tiny earthquake—*seaquake?*—woke them all at what was probably dawn on the surface. Pebbles fell on the skiff, but nothing more seemed to happen.

The external lights cast shadows in front of them, and Donal maneuvered them just a little further in to look ... and found that the old lava tube they were in had been much wider ahead. They had a lively discussion over breakfast before unanimously agreeing to go a little further in.

Unanimity lasted until the tube in front of them split.

"We need breadcrumbs," Jes announced.

"Breadcrumbs float away," Chris pointed out.

Jes scowled. "You know what I mean. We need to mark the path we take."

Amalia fingered the hilt of her sword. "But then people could follow us."

Jes threw up her hands. "Amalia, you are so paranoid! Who's going to follow us *here*?"

"Bad people," Amalia said ominously. "Spies. Maybe pirates." She glanced over at Mrs. Clemens. "No offense."

"None taken." Mrs. Clemens smiled. "Some pi—people use codes for just that reason. Mark your path without giving away which one it is because you mark the others, too."

That sounded somewhere between sensible and brilliant. Donal nodded. "The external arm can mark the entrances. We can mark the first five choices with our initials in order of age—M for Mrs. Clemens—then back is S for sea monster, ahead is T for treasure, not taken is L for Lava. So, the one we just came through is MS, and we have to decide which will be MT and which ML."

"Stick to bigger places. The people who left the treasure probably had to be able to turn around," Chris advised.

It only took a few moments to mark them. The tunnel on their left was definitely the smaller of the two options, so they took the tunnel straight ahead.

Some chambers had only one way out and didn't have to be marked. Still, they had gone through A, D, and J with only C for Chris remaining when they reached an immense cavern that could have held a fleet of ships. The wreckage of an ancient frigate was at one end upon a sandy beach. Bizarrely, the chamber opened up into air. Multiple tunnels led away from the beach, all apparently above water.

"Oh, man. Do you know what this means?" Chris asked.

"Amazing discoveries," Donal answered.

"The translations were right," Jes added.

"Room for sword practice!" Amalia crowed.

They all looked at Chris, enjoying his look of frustration, until Mrs. Clemens took pity on him.

"And perhaps treasure, too."

The cavern was enormous. The lights of the skiff had only been able to illuminate it partially, but Donal guessed that it was perhaps a thousand yards long and half that wide. The walls curved up into a ceiling about fifty yards above them. A chimney-like opening at the far end held a suggestion of daylight and explained the fresh air. There were no stalactites or stalagmites coming down from the ceiling or up from the water. This cavern had been carved by lava, not water.

The old ship on the beach was too close to ignore—and, as Chris was quick to point out, its sailors might have had a treasure map with them. The ship was surprisingly intact, suggesting that the tunnels had once been partially above water, allowing it to sail or row its way in. Their torches glinted off the walls and the water, adding a general sense of dim light to the cavern. Given the lack of lava, the chimney had to open up high in the wall of the caldera. Donal imagined that they were in a vase next to a soup bowl, so that when the soup bowl's lava overflowed, it couldn't get up high enough to enter the vase of their cavern.

The closer they got, the older the ship looked. The shape was wrong for a frigate, and there were no openings for canons. "Were there ships before gunpowder was invented?" Amalia asked, fingering the hilt of her sword.

"Long before gunpowder," Mrs. Clemens assured her. "There were ships before people learned how to work metal at all."

"If they couldn't get out, there may be bodies inside," Chris pointed out. He sounded very cheerful about the possibility, and Donal noticed that only Jes looked disturbed.

"Skeletons at worst after all this time," Donal countered, looking at Jes. She smiled crookedly, as though she knew he was trying to make her feel better.

The ropes along the side had rotted away, but a hole in the prow allowed them to walk right into the ship's hold. Wooden bunks, a little small even for them, lined the walls while tattered remains of hammocks hung from the low ceiling. A few broken barrels—all wood, with wooden hoops instead of metal—were broken open on the floor, the contents long gone. A tarnished bronze bell hung from a peg near a ladder headed up, and Chris rapped it with the hilt of his sword. The gong was hollow but echoing.

"Chris!" Amalia hissed. "Don't let people know we're here!"

Chris shrugged. "There's nobody here but us."

"Maybe." Donal bent closer to the ladder. "But someone has been here since this ship was abandoned. This rung gave way in the last few years—where it splintered, the wood hasn't turned grey yet."

They crowded around to look. Mrs. Clemens nodded. "It's sheltered from weather here, so it might take a decade or more for this to weather, but I agree that it can't have been centuries."

Donal carefully climbed the ladder up to the deck. The other rungs all held. The torchlight was brighter with the reflections from walls and water, and he pointed out something on the deck. "I'm not sure how long dried blood stays brown, but I'm pretty sure it's not centuries."

A footprint—adult, male by the size—was outlined in old blood on the empty deck.

Mrs. Clemens said something that sounded like a curse, if Donal had known the language, but offered no other comments. The other three gathered round and looked at the footprint. There were no others, so presumably the person had either bandaged their foot or put on a shoe.

"Whatever treasure this ship had carried is gone now," Chris complained. He brightened, smiling. "Unless they all died before they could get it to the ship!"

Jes glowered at him before going up to the front of the boat. "Look, there's one of those things you have Donal, with the squiggly lines."

A bronze sextant sat beside a fancy bronze compass by the ship's wheel. Donal was staring at the sextant, noting that the script was different, when Jes crowed. "It's in ancient Kesch! This is amazing! A bronze age ship from more than a thousand leagues away!"

They meant to go home again. Did they make it? Was there more than one ship?

The ship had a name, engraved on a brass plaque on the ship's wheel. Jes frowned at it for a few minutes as the others continued to look around. "It's something like the Western Horizon. Sun-Down-Sea. We're certainly west of ancient Kesch, so maybe it was made and named specifically for this trip."

Bones didn't generally bother Donal, but he was glad they hadn't found any bodies on the boat.

It was sad enough if this trip had been the ship's entire purpose, and it had ended up stranded and broken here.

There was a small splashing sound behind them, and Donal whirled, looking at the water. No ripples remained, and the shadowy depths probably held nothing but fish. Still, the footprint wasn't from the bronze age. Donal straightened up. It was harder telling other people what to do when he wasn't on board the skiff, but someone had to say the obvious.

"I don't think we should leave the skiff unguarded. Let's go back and make a fire so we can see better in here."

Jes and Chris started a fire on the beach with old wood that tides or prior explorers had brought in. Donal, with help from Amalia and Mrs. Clemens, set up a very basic weapon for the skiff—an electric shock along its surface. Along the way, he set up a few safe guards. The footprint, and that splash, had him ... cautious. Not spooked, not paranoid, just cautious.

Donal put on the new light filtering goggles that Jes had given him. Facing the fire, the glare was minimized so that he could still see clearly. Away from the fire, he changed the filters, and he could see by the tiny lights of shells embedded in the walls and from the firelight reflecting from the water. He looked out to the cavern, jumping a little at a small sound of rock hitting rock, but there was nothing to see except still water and a shrinking cone of dim light near the top.

Time to focus.

"I'd like to do some exploring and mapping, but someone should stay with the ship, just in case. Mrs. Clemens, if you'd watch the ship, I think the rest of us can split into groups of two with one leading and one mapping. Why don't we meet back here in an hour?"

Donal tried not to hold his breath. He never took charge like this, but no one was objecting.

"I'll go with you," Amalia offered, "and Chris can go with Jes, so each pair has someone with a sword. Mrs. Clemens, did you bring a sword? I packed a spare."

Mrs. Clemens smiled. "I'm all set, Your Highness, but thank you."

Amalia frowned. "I think we had better drop all those titles. Captain is okay, because that's Donal, but all of us are 'Your Highness'. Could you use our first names since we're all crewmates?"

"Please," Chris agreed. "I only get 'Your Highness'

when I'm in trouble."

"And I'm on vacation," Jes added. "Someone else is looking after our people right now. I'd like to be Jes, too."

Mrs. Clemens smiled. "Would you like to call me Grace?"

They all blinked, and Donal wondered if the others felt as horrified as he did. "Let's do one change at a time," he said.

Since he was wearing the light filtering goggles, he handed off the night vision glasses to Amalia. The distance goggles he handed to Jes, trusting her and Chris to work out who would wear them.

Donal and Amalia took the tunnel furthest to the left, while Jes and Chris took the one furthest to the right. Chris held a torch aloft in one hand, his sword in the other, while Jes had paper and charcoal for mapping and marking.

Amalia, who didn't need a torch, took one piece of charcoal. She touched her sword occasionally but kept it sheathed. Donal took paper and charcoal for mapping, just able to make out the paper and tunnel with the special lenses.

The first side tunnel, on their right, led back to

the clearing through the second tunnel there. Donal shifted his glasses and waved to Mrs. Clemens while Amalia stayed inside to avoid hurting her night vision. The next side tunnel was on the left and slanted up for a while before opening into a narrow hall of marble statues. Pigment on the walls made incomprehensible pictures. Writing like the script on the map covered a section of one wall, and Donal copied it down carefully.

"Are they ... people? I mean, they must be people because they had art and writing, but look at the statues. They don't quite look human." Amalia stared, pointing. "Are these the people who created the islands?"

Donal looked at the statues. They all had six fingers, with a trace of webbing between them, no hair on their heads, and narrow, flattened features. They looked too human to be anything else. At the same time, no humans he had ever met, near or far, looked like these. Hair texture, or skin color, might have given some clue to where in the world they had originated from, but neither were apparent. Were they naturally hairless, or did the lack of hair have significance? Did they look like the people who had carved them, or were they how these people had imagined their gods appeared?

"I wish I could draw well enough to show what these look like," Donal sighed. "They're too heavy to move."

Amalia shrugged. "Hand over some paper. I don't do sword practice *all* day." She paused, thinking. "Okay, not all day, *every* day."

Her sketches were good, but their time was passing. They agreed to press on for five more minutes before turning back. The tunnel turned to the right, back to the left, then to the right again until it was impossible to tell what direction they were actually going. Donal was about to suggest that they head back when Amalia stopped, one hand up.

"There's something up ahead," she hissed. She passed back her charcoal and drew her sword.

"Don't just stab it—it might be Chris and Jes!" Donal whispered back.

Donal wasn't sure, but he thought that Amalia rolled her eyes behind the glasses. She stepped forward quietly, and Donal followed behind.

He could hear what she was hearing now, a muted duh-dump, as if someone dragging a bad leg. It was too loud for Jes, who was practically silent in her boots, and too quiet for Christopher. They crept closer, then Amalia flung herself around a corner and immediately screamed.

Donal sprinted forward. It was impossibly bright, and he switched the filters on his glasses so he could see. Amalia had her eyes covered from the pain of the sudden light of the fire on the beach through the night vision. In front of her was a slender dark blue figure that inched along the sand towards them, planting its front feet and pulling its body behind it. Donal gasped, and the creature looked up through enormous green eyes.

"Blot?"

"Blah!" the hatchling replied happily, surging forward to snuggle against Donal's feet.

"But—your father! Your siblings! You ..." Donal sighed and reached down to rub the little head. "You're mine now, aren't you, Blot?"

"Blah," Blot crooned.

Blot followed them back to the water and the skiff. He seemed delighted to rub up to the skiff once he knew Donal was going to be in it.

"Mrs. Clemens didn't rush out when you

screamed," Donal whispered softly to Amalia. "Something may be wrong."

Amalia, the dark vision goggles perched on her head, nodded her understanding and grasped her sword in its sheath. "I'll go first," she whispered back. She took a a few more steps, then called out "I'm back."

She swung into the skiff, then stopped so quickly that Donal had to grab the wall not to run into her.

In front of them, Mrs. Clemens had a black powder pistol in her right hand and a dagger in her left. Both were pointed at a ragged, bearded man on the floor in front of her. "Oh, good," she said cheerfully. "You're unharmed. That means I won't have to kill him."

Amalia had the man blindfolded and tied up before Donal had even seen his face. A rag—torn from his shirt, by the look of it—was bound around the man's right foot, confirming that he was the source of the footprint they'd found.

Chris and Jes showed up just as Amalia finished. They were arguing about plans for further exploring but fell silent at a gesture from Amalia.

"Who is that?" Chris asked.

"I'm just an unfortunate traveler," the man began.

Mrs. Clemens kicked him. "He's a pirate."

"Are you sure?" Donal asked.

Mrs. Clemens looked at Donal, then at the others. "I'm sure."

Donal sighed. "Then what do we do with him? Has he done things so terrible we need to kill him? Or bad enough that we have to take him in to justice?"

The man squirmed in his bonds but didn't answer. Mrs. Clemens hesitated. "For the first, I don't think so. Yet. For the second, I don't know. I know that you can't believe a word that comes out of his mouth."

When a quiet grandmother becomes an avenging angel of death, it's probably good to pay attention. Donal bit his lip. "Either he has a way out of here, or he'll die if we leave him here. If he has a way out, he's dangerous. If he doesn't have a way out, he's more dangerous."

Amalia nodded. "Killing him is the easiest way, but you know our parents would be upset. I'd probably get grounded. Leaving him here to escape or die is a little better, but Jes would probably get upset. Taking him to justice is dangerous, but our parents won't be mad. Letting him go … Well, that might work, but if he's an idiot like Mathis, he might decide we wronged him and come wreck something."

"I'm not an idiot," the man interjected. "Definitely not that much of an idiot." He paused. "I am really, really thirsty, though. Do you have any fresh water? Or ale?"

Donal hesitated a moment. A prisoner was as much of a responsibility as a pet, and he liked Blot much better than the pirate. Still … human beings shared water. He took a cup and water flagon from the stores, then held the brimming cup to the man's lips. The man drank eagerly, then settled back with a sigh.

Curious despite himself, Donal pulled off the blindfold. The man looked older than Donal's mother, maybe a bit younger than Mrs. Clemens. He had straggly brown hair with a few streaks of gray, a ragged brown beard, and blue eyes.

The man's eyes widened now. He straightened. "You look just like your mother."

Donal frowned. "How do you know my mother?"

The man gave a mirthless laugh. "We were married for about six months. You're my son, Donal."

The initial impulse, to strike him or gag him or let Amalia kill him, Donal suppressed. Instead, he turned and walked out of the skiff and sat at the water's edge, Blot's head on his lap.

Chris was the first one to come try to talk to him. "I'm sure he's lying."

"I'm sure he is." Donal was not at all sure, but it felt good to say it. "What did you and Jes find?"

"The first and second tunnels are dead ends, and the third keeps going further than we could follow in just an hour. We'll start there later. How about you?"

"Marble statues, strange pictures, lots more strange writing. I took notes, and Amalia made sketches."

Blot chose that moment to snuggle closer, and Chris jumped. "Wait, is that ...?"

Donal smiled. "Yes, this is Blot. He followed me." Donal closed his eyes and tipped back his head. His smile became crooked. "You know, if that *was* my father, I've already given him more care—and felt more responsibility for him—then he ever did for me. Ten years. I can't abandon a baby sea monster. Who could abandon a baby?"

Chris shook his head. "Well, good thing he's lying. But maybe some people are like the mother sea monsters. They make the baby and then have faith that someone else will do a better job of raising it than they could. And seriously, you have your mom *and* your uncle. Not many people have parents that good, parents who understand them and support them in who they really are."

Donal smiled again. "You do a lot of thinking for a force of destruction."

Chris smiled back. "You're pretty brave for an inventor."

It felt like a bonding moment, minus the punching he sometimes saw boys doing when they talked about emotions. Donal decided he was good with that.

They took turns fishing until supper, to stretch the supplies to cover two more. Another tremor shook the chamber as they cleaned the fish. Stones up to the size of their fists fell into the water. Blot happily watched the fish rise to these ripples and caught most of his own supper.

They fed the man before interrogating him. It was less effective, they agreed, but more humane. If they weren't going to kill him, torture was out.

"You can call me Robert," he said. "It's not the name I was born with, but I'm no longer sure which one that was."

His first story, that he'd washed up here, was stared out of him. His second, that he'd been marooned by enemies, was treated with the same silent contempt. They knew how hard this place was to reach.

His third story might—*might*—have been true. "There were rumors about this volcano, that there was something inside. It was quiet when I got here a few weeks ago. I scaled the peak, worked my way down with ropes with two others. Three days after we started, the ground rumbled, and gas came up from the caldera. I made it to an inactive lava tube. The other two didn't. I had to travel a while to avoid the gas and the heat. When I tried to go back, the passage had collapsed." He shrugged. "With heat and steam and smoke coming up, the ship may have waited a couple of days to see if we'd make it out, but they wouldn't have waited longer. There's no fresh water here, and the two flagons I had are bone dry. This place is a death sentence if you can't get out. Even if I made it to the surface, it's weeks by raft to the nearest land, and how would I make a raft? I thought I'd steal your craft and drop the people in it off on the nearest unpopulated island, no harm done."

"For a sufficiently narrow definition of 'harm,'"

Mrs. Clemens said. "And what was supposed to be here?"

Robert shrugged. "Treasure, of some kind. You never know, with treasure. One person's find of the century is another's disappointment. Usually, if you can find the right person to sell it to, you can still make money." He leaned forward, still bound. "I could help you find it."

"No, thank you," Donal said. "First, we have to arrange a place to keep you until we're ready to leave."

Robert went from charming to serious in a breath. "If you're not going to take me with you, kill me before you go. Thirst is a horrible way to die."

Donal tilted his head slightly. "You're counting on us not being able to bring ourselves to kill you, aren't you?"

Robert nodded. "Right now, those are the best odds I have."

A stake buried in rock, feet chained together and to the stake with enough slack to walk a few paces or lie down, and hands chained together six inches apart from each other started Donal's plan.

Amalia added in a few booby traps around the area, careful that Blot could not set them off. Last, Donal set a reprogrammed Zap on guard.

They set up guard shifts, anyway, but further away. Zap turned out to be enough. Half an hour after they left Robert alone, Donal could hear Zap responding to the pirate's behavior.

"Desist from attempting to escape. Shock in ten ... nine ... eight ... *zap.*"

There were muttered curses from Robert, and Zap spoke again. "Next shock will be at a higher setting. Please rest and desist before you are injured."

Donal realized as he settled down to his watch that he hadn't needed Zap for himself the entire trip. There was so much to do in the moment. He hadn't had time to get lost in a project when every day was an adventure.

Blot curled up beside him, and Donal listened to the water lapping and dripping, Zap making his rounds, and the pirate grumbling. Life was good.

Mrs. Clemens volunteered to stay at the camp again, and Donal thought she likely would have insisted if they'd tried to argue with her. He didn't try; he'd talked to her earlier, while the others were eating, and she knew about the safeguards he'd added.

Amalia was not as easily convinced. "Have you ever killed anyone?" she asked the housekeeper.

Mrs. Clemens shook her head, but not necessarily in denial. "That's not a thing to be proud of, Your—Amalia, nor necessarily a thing to be ashamed of either. I can do what's needed. I'd rather that none of you have to make that choice."

They split up again, this time Chris with Donal and Amalia with Jes. They flipped a coin to see who would get which side, and Jes got the side she and Chris had been on the first time. They set a meeting time of three hours, hoping to get as much seen as possible.

Amalia turned down the night vision goggles, so Chris picked them up. Jes stayed with the magnification goggles, and Donal with the filtered ones. That meant Amalia would carry a torch in her off hand while Jes kept the notes.

Donal and Chris started on the fourth tunnel from the left, which went a satisfying distance back into the base of the caldera. Donal touched the wall frequently, to make sure it wasn't going too close to active lava.

They finally came to a fork in the wall, with one tunnel going right and the other continuing on straight. They paused to discuss which way to go, and then Donal tilted his head, listening. He gestured to Chris, who listened, too.

"Sounds like one set of footsteps. Hopefully Amalia, with Jes behind and too quiet to hear."

They waited, Chris with his sword out and ready. In another minute, a glimmer of light shone down the tunnel, and Chris flipped up the night vision goggles. Donal set his to normal vision and took out a spare torch.

Amalia nodded to them as she turned the corner. "So, none of the others go this far back. We may want to check them out, if there's time, but I have a feeling this is the important one."

Donal stepped up to light his torch with hers, then handed it over to Chris. "Where's Jes?"

Amalia whirled around. "She's so quiet, I didn't even notice that she wasn't with me. I'd better go back."

"No need." Jes came around the corner, grinning.

"The things you can see with these!"

"Come on," Amalia pointed. "More adventure awaits."

The walls were no longer cool, but not quite warm. Donal kept one hand on them when he wasn't mapping their route.

The tunnel slowly changed, looking shaped instead of formed by nature. After a bit, they came to a wider area, with writing on both sides on the walls. Six fingered hands carved from stone pulled back stone curtains. Jes went to examine them while Donal copied down the writing.

"These are real hands. I mean, they were sculpted based on real models. Finger lengths, breadths, scars—each one is unique."

"That argues against the imagined gods theory," Amalia commented

Through the carved curtains, the next room had statues that looked like children. There was more writing on the walls, and among the dozens of unique sculptures, Amalia pointed out one that was different.

"Look. This one has five fingers and hair and features that look more ... typical."

"They considered that child the same as the others." Donal nodded. "Adopted or born to them, that child was theirs, too."

The walls were getting warmer as they pushed on, and then they stopped. A huge open space was before them, with stairs that led up and across and down again.

The stairs were not anchored to anything. Each hung in the air, separate, impossible.

Jes swallowed. "I don't like this at all."

Chris made a weird sound in his throat. "I don't like this, and I jump out of second story windows into water every day. But I also don't want to stop."

Donal looked at it. Reversing gravity was theoretically possible if you could find enough elements that violated all known physical laws. Science changed all the time. Taking a breath, he stepped onto the first step.

The step plummeted down six feet.

"No problem. This is what rope is for." Amalia pulled out her pack and wrestled out a coil of rope. "I'll lower myself down to you and help you back up."

She anchored it around Chris and Jes and then let the rope out slowly through her hands. She reached the step, then grabbed the rope with both hands as the step rose two feet back up.

"I was not expecting that." She paused, looking at Donal. "What if instead of booby-traps for bad people, they had helpful things for nice people?"

"People who stay together?" Donal guessed. He bit his lip, frowning. "It's possible. To find out, one of the others would have to come down."

Jes put one hand over her eyes. "I can do it. And Chris is stronger if we have to be pulled back up."

Donal remembered that Jes was horribly afraid of heights, but it didn't seem like a good time to mention it. "Okay, we've got you."

Jes lowered herself down from the edge, and the other two caught her legs and helped her the last bit. As soon as her feet touched, the step came up even with the edge.

"Last chance to be sensible," Chris said cheerfully. "Oops. There it goes." He jumped onto the step, which immediately rose to the level of the next step.

"On three?" Donal suggested. "One, two ..."

On three, they stepped across together. The step rose immediately to the level of the next, and so on, block by block, until they began going down again. When they got off at last, still together, Jes gave a little sigh.

"I hope the rest of this has anti-booby-traps like this. If they were set up the way Amalia and Donal protect spaces ..."

"Oh, I think we'd already be dead by now," Chris reassured her.

The chamber beyond the floating stairs felt sad to Donal. It seemed silly, but the pictures on the walls seemed to show, not people setting out for something new, but people leaving. There were no children in the picture, and the objects left behind by the people looked somehow forlorn.

"They're not coming back," he said, pointing to an object left behind in the picture. It was made of crystal, but it was clearly a sextant. *A tool to find your way home.*

"Where did they go?" Jes asked. "Why did they leave?"

"I don't know," Donal said. "Maybe this wasn't the right place for them. Maybe they had done what they were here to do." He looked at the picture again. "I think maybe the children stayed. But not here. Just ... closer than wherever the rest went."

"I don't suppose we'll ever know." Jes sounded as sad as he felt. "It will take lifetimes just to decipher the script you've copied down."

They went on more quietly to the next room, and then Chris let out a war cry that might have been heard back at the skiff. The room was full of baskets of jewels, gold, and strange crystal sheets that weighed almost nothing but were covered with writing.

Donal found intricately carved shapes of the people, some with sea monsters. Amalia found a small disc that hovered in the air without moving. Jes started crying when she found a crystal sheet that had writing in three scripts—Old Dornish, ancient Kuesh, and the script that was on everything else.

The chamber shook with another tremor. Suddenly, there was the smell of sulfur. Donal rested his hand against the wall, and snatched it back, blowing on it. "We're too close. We need to go back."

"But ... the treasure!"

"You have fifteen minutes to pack up only what you can carry. If the volcano calms down, we might be able to come back for more."

Jes dumped out her backpack and slid crystal sheets into it, starting with the one in the three languages. Donal took carvings and small paintings, anything that showed the people of these times, but he kept his supplies. Getting back was most important. Amalia grabbed technology, and Donal trusted that she would share when they were safely home. Chris took jewels and gold.

Another tremor hit before their fifteen minutes were up, and Donal raised his hand. "That's it," he said. "We're done."

No one argued. They raced through the leaving chamber and back to the stairs. Pieces of the ceiling rained down around them as they kept their gait carefully synchronized. Step together, up, step together, up. A rock hit the step they were on, and they grabbed at each other to keep their balance. Another step up, and another, and then down the other side as chunks of rock crashed down beside them. Jes almost teetered backwards as they finally reached the level floor, but they grabbed her, and Amalia took her hand as they ran.

They ran through the earlier chambers, still dodging falling rock, and Jes cried out as one of the stone curtains broke apart. Chris, in the lead, took the route that he and Donal had traveled from the ship, and the others followed. A tremor shook them, then another, and another.

"We need to get out, all the way out. With this many quakes, the volcano is going to blow, and that could block us all in here." Donal shook his head. "I should have suggested we leave when we felt the earlier ones."

Amalia snorted. "We would have talked you out of it. So, we just get Blot and Robert on board and leave. And if there isn't room for both, I say we take Blot."

"Mrs. Clemens will be ready to leave when we get there," Jes reassured him. "She's wonderful in a crisis. Let me just go ahead and wave to her that we're coming."

Amalia took Jes's pack, and Jes sped away as they carried on in silence. Too soon, she was back.

"We've got a problem," Jes said, catching her breath. "Robert has captured Mrs. Clemens."

"How did he get past Zap?" Donal wondered.

"How did he get the drop on Mrs. Clemens?" Jes countered. "Either he's got an accomplice, or he's got a trick we don't know about."

"I knew I should have put up more booby-traps!" Amalia grumbled. "He may just steal the skiff and leave us here to die."

Donal didn't mention that she'd just proposed doing the same to him. "We're got to focus on what tricks *we* have that *he* doesn't know about. In the meantime, he's not going anywhere. I put a lot of safeguards on the skiff before I left. Not only can he not fly it, Mrs. Clemens can't fly it if we're not there."

"Does Mrs. Clemens know that?" Jes demanded.

Donal nodded. "She approved of the idea."

Jes eased back. "Okay, then. We just need to rescue her, disarm him, get everybody on the skiff, and escape before the volcano erupts." Another tremor punctuated her assessment. "No pressure."

"None at all," Donal agreed. "I've got a plan."

One of the great things about the alchemical fire extinguisher was that it made a fire blaze brilliantly for about twenty seconds and then go out. That had been easy enough to do back home in the library, but while this was a bigger fire, it would go out just as well if they could just get the extinguisher into it without being seen.

Donal handed Jes two of the black pellets from his pouch. One would do the job, but it wasn't worth risking failure if she just missed the fire with her first toss. With the fire on the beach the only major source of light in the undersea cavern, the bright light would destroy Robert's night vision while Amalia and Chris as their two fighters would have the night vison goggles and the low light filtered goggles to put on immediately after. Jes would sneak silently near to the fire to throw in the black pellet, and that would be the signal for the fighters to attack.

Donal would be the bait.

He watched with the far vision goggles until the others were in place and then took a deep breath. *I hate conflict. I hate raised voices, even mine. But my friends are counting on me, and I can do this.*

He marched directly into the camp so that he stood across the fire from the skiff. "Robert, you snake-bitten peddler of lies, what kind of a father do you claim to be? You abandon me before I'm even born, you lie more easily than you breathe, and now you steal my submersible? You aren't worthy to be called human. You aren't even worthy to be called scum."

Robert came around the side of the skiff, a gun held to Mrs. Clemens's temple. For one moment Donal was distracted by his appearance. He'd shaved off his beard, or maybe Mrs. Clemens had done it for him, and he looked like a pirate now instead of a prisoner. He looked like someone that a woman—maybe not his mother, but some woman—would notice.

"So, you did get something from me," Robert

chuckled although Donal saw that his eyes were tight. "Your mother wouldn't lose control of her temper if a cow ate her dress with her in it." Mrs. Clemens jerked at his grasp despite the gun to her forehead, and Robert swore. "Grace, so help me I will splatter your brains on this beach."

"You leave my mother out of this, you maggot-infested reject from a dung heap! You aren't fit to speak her name. You aren't fit to speak my crew member's name either. She's easily worth twenty of you."

"Hard to argue that," Robert conceded. "But I'm the one with the gun."

"How *could* you?" Donal asked. He sounded angry rather than hurt. To his surprise, he *was* angry, not hurt.

"Sorry, Donal. Nothing personal."

"Is that supposed to make it *better?* Nothing *personal?*"

Robert was turning his attention from Mrs. Clemens to Donal, just as he'd hoped. Mrs. Clemens, unfortunately, didn't seem to agree with this part of the plan. She stomped down hard on Robert's foot and wrenched herself away from him, blocking Robert from Donal ... but also blocking Robert's gaze from the fire. "You want to shoot me, Robert, you go right ahead."

Robert held the gun out in front of him pointed towards her and snarled. Donal moved quickly to his right, so that the pirate would once again be facing him across the light. "Or you could just shoot me. It couldn't make you a worse father than you already are."

Robert made a sound that was like a scream, threw the pistol on the ground, and reached out to Mrs. Clemens with his bare hands.

The fire blazed bright—*Jes has great timing*—and Robert screamed again, louder. Donal covered his eyes, threw himself to the ground, and called, "Blot!"

The fire burned out, then there was a surprised sound from Robert, followed by a strangled cry. A few moments later, Blot was licking Donal's face.

It was very, very dark, but he could make out three figures his height standing over a fourth, larger figure on the ground. A tremor struck, and Donal cleared his throat. "Everybody into the skiff. Tie up Robert and bring him if there's room." He struggled to his feet. "Come, Blot."

"Bluh!" the hatchling agreed.

Jes raced in from the darkness while the others followed, dragging Robert between them. He didn't appear to be conscious, but Donal wasn't going to spare any worry for him. It took Donal a moment to undo the safeguards he'd put in place, then he slid into the pilot's seat and put his hand on the thermal reader, letting it verify his identity. He flipped switches up, starting the engine and turning on the lights.

With the lights on Donal could confirm that Blot had grown since morning, from the thickness of Donal's arm to the thickness of his upper leg and twice as long. "Can you curl up, Blot, so we don't have to kill Robert?"

"There's less food and more room," Mrs. Clemens said. "Sorry, Captain. It won't happen again."

"It wasn't your fault," Donal offered.

Mrs. Clemens shook her head. "It completely was. But we'll talk about that later."

Zap, battered but fixable, was by his chair. Amalia had dragged in their packs, and everyone except Blot and Robert were properly strapped in. Robert appeared to be regaining consciousness, but it was his concern for Blot that made Donal cautious as he took the skiff back out into the water.

Tremor after tremor shook the cavern, and Donal steered into the first tunnel. The water was choppy, pushing the skiff back and forth and scraping them against the sides. One falling rock dented the skiff as he hurried to follow the tunnel marked JS, and they had to fight a current to enter the tunnel marked AS. They burst out of that tunnel, as the roof of it collapsed, into a larger chamber where falling rocks obscured the markings.

Donal focused his gaze on the markings of the three remaining tunnels. As his view of one tunnel cleared enough to read DL, he moved the skiff to face between the two remaining, focusing just on the visual clues. A larger quake hit, moving the walls of one tunnel further apart so that the DS on one side was finally visible. He took the tunnel even as it began to close again.

"Faster, faster, faster," Jes chanted, her hand on the console as though on the throttle. Donal turned the skiff sideways through the newly narrowed passage, wincing at Blot's soft cry.

One more turn into the tunnel marked MS,

then a quick adjustment almost straight up, and they were clear. Lava was flowing into the water behind them, and Donal gulped as he saw one stream shower over the tunnel they had just left.

"There might be a way back in, someday," Jes said softly.

Donal shrugged. "Maybe. Maybe some things belong in the past. We're lucky to have escaped with what we did. Knowledge, bragging rights, and our lives."

Robert groaned, and there was a thud as Mrs. Clemens kicked him.

The water was teeming with sea life, all fleeing.

They dodged a giant squid, maneuvered around a pod of dolphins, and ended up inside a school of silver fish half the size of the skiff. Waves were muted under the water, but molten boulders came down around them from time to time,

A green sea monster larger than Blot's father grabbed at them among the silver fish, and Donal braced. "Hold on!"

"Not again!" Amalia cried.

"Not quite." Donal hit the switch he'd installed the day before, and a shock went through the monster, making it twitch and drop them. They dropped below the level of the silver fish, who scattered and reformed further away. "As soon as we're a few miles further out, we'll take to the air. But we're pretty safe in the meantime."

"Unless we run out of food for Blot," Chris griped. "He's eating more than I do!"

"I think I can see him growing," Amalia chimed in. "No, Blot, the dictionaries are NOT food!"

Jes twisted around in her seat to take the dictionaries onto her lap. "Hand me my pack, could you? I've got work to do."

Donal watched as she pored over the crystal sheet with the three kinds of writing on it. It looked boring to him, but he remembered what it felt like putting together an invention. *That must be how Amalia feels about sword practice or how Chris feels about running and climbing. What you love doing is never boring.*

He dodged another boulder. In the air it would have been impossible, but the water slowed it down. It was getting longer between falling rocks and other disasters, but piloting still needed his full attention. *I don't see how anyone could ever be bored under the water.* Donal paused, remembering the night sky, lit with a thousand stars. *How could you possibly choose if you could only have one?*

They took to the air as soon as they'd gone five minutes without falling rocks. Jes moved to the seat behind Donal's and kept working on the translations while Amalia came up to help navigate and Chris continued to feed Blot. Mrs. Clemens watched Robert, her kind face grim.

They searched Donal's maps, and the closest inhabited island was a six-hour detour to the South. Unfortunately, that was long enough that Blot had eaten every bit of meat on board by the time they got there, and he was starting to express interest in the leather of their shoes. The island looked tiny from the air and wasn't much bigger after they had landed. There was a small fishing village on one side, and Mrs. Clemens reported that a ship docked every week or two with mail or to pick up or drop off passengers. The far side where they set down was at least a half day walk through jungle from the village.

Donal escorted Robert out under the watchful eye and weapons of Mrs. Clemens.

"I'm not doing this to be nice. I'm doing this to spare my mother embarrassment. If you ever show up anywhere near the Waveborn islands again, you will be charged with piracy, attempted regicide, and treason. Do we understand each other?"

Robert looked like he wanted to argue some part of that—probably regicide since Donal wasn't actually a king. Wisely, he kept his mouth shut and nodded.

Donal tilted his head. He couldn't see anything of this man in himself and didn't want him in his life, but one curiosity nagged at him. "Are you actually my father? Or was that just one of your lies?"

An expression of … regret? … crossed the pirate's face, and he looked away. "I'm sorry, lad. I'm not your father. A father doesn't leave and never look back. Any man worth knowing would be proud to have you as a son."

Donal nodded briskly and handed over a small pouch. "That should be enough to get you some distance away. Keep going. Make something worthwhile out of your life, so someone actually cares when you're gone."

He turned back to the skiff, walking by Mrs. Clemens with her loaded pistol and grim expression. He rubbed Blot's head before returning to the captain's chair. When Mrs. Clemens was back inside, he waited only for her to strap in before taking off.

They were out of sight of the island when Donal finally spoke again. "Mrs. Clemens, did Robert ever use the last name Clemens?"

The housekeeper paused. "He did."

"You let him take you hostage to see if he would, didn't you?"

Mrs. Clemens sighed. "I took the firing pin out, first. I had a dagger under my skirt to take him with if he tried to fire it, but he didn't. He threatened it, but he couldn't seem to go through with it, and when I tried to force his hand—well, you saw what he did instead."

"He called you Grace," Donal explained. "We never did, and I didn't think it would have come up while you were guarding him."

"I thought you were widowed!" Jes exclaimed.

Mrs. Clemens smiled although it was crooked. "Legally, I am. After two years missing at sea, a spouse is considered dead. I don't think Clemens was ever his legal name, anyway. It was a long, long time ago."

Donal nodded. "Do you know if he's my father?"

The housekeeper shook her head. "I never met your mother's husband. It was a brief marriage."

That was an understatement. Donal nodded again. "He said he wasn't."

"That settles it. He isn't your father." Chris sounded cheerfully certain.

Donal shook his head. "Maybe. But most people have tells when they lie, little signs that they're not being honest. My mom twists her sleeve when she isn't telling the whole truth. She was doing that when she pretended not to be worried about our trip. Robert looks you straight in the eye when he lies. When he said he wasn't my father, he looked away."

"So, how do you know?" Jes asked softly.

Donal smiled. "I don't. But it doesn't matter, any more than it matters who Blot's mother was. Blot has me now, and I have my mom and Uncle Keegan and all of you."

"Are you going to tell your mom?" Amalia asked.

Donal was silent for a while, thinking. Blot squeezed in next to his chair and rubbed against Donal's leg.

"I don't lie to my mother. If she asks me if I met a man who said he was my father, I'd have to say yes. But I think Blot and the treasure and the erupting volcano are the important things here." Donal looked down at Blot, who was at least a foot longer already. "And right now, it's time to go under water and give Blot some room to swim."

The trip under water was slower, especially as they had to surface to check the sextant against the stars. A pod of orcas took a brief interest in Blot but retreated after an electric shock from the skiff. Blot kept up easily, even catching his own fish. Sometimes he curled around the skiff and held on as they traveled, making happy noises.

Jes used almost every minute on the translations, turning down even chances to pilot the skiff. She had to be reminded to eat, and for the first time, Donal got a glimpse of what he was like when he was enthralled with a project. When she started to sneak a small light to keep working when it was her turn to sleep, Donal used Captain's privilege to bring her up to the co-pilot chair.

"I know it's hard to take a break when you're making progress," he said softly. "But your body and your mind both need rest. If you need me to, I can program Zap to stop you when you've gone too long without a break. That's what I use at home."

He watched the sea outside them instead of her face, but he heard her sigh. It sounded like he imagined his always did.

"All right," Jes agreed. "But—I'm almost sure what it says, and I can't wait to tell you all, but I have to know that I'm right."

Donal nodded. "Those crystal sheets—those belong to you. You rescued them. Nobody is going to take them away from you unless you decide to loan them out to scientists. You have time. The mysteries have been there for centuries. A couple of hours more is okay."

Jes laughed a little, muffled with her hand to keep from waking the others. "I'll try to remember that. Why don't I steer for a couple of hours, then I'll get some sleep?"

Donal turned over the controls to her, then

watched Blot until his eyes began to close. *I'm becoming more like my mother. I think I'm happy about that.*

By morning they were close enough to message home that they were safe and well and on their way back. "We've got a surprise, so we'll be coming in through the sea tunnel. I'll let you know when we're a few hours out," Donal told his mother.

"We'll be waiting for you. Anything you'll need besides food and then baths and a good night's sleep?" Donal's mother sounded happy but also relieved. It felt nice to know he had been missed.

"Just you, although we won't say no to hot food. Oh … maybe fifty pounds of raw fish?"

The others were staring at him when he signed off. "Fifty pounds of raw fish and she didn't even ask you why?" Chris asked.

"My mom's pretty cool," Donal admitted.

Amalia snorted. "All of our parents are pretty cool. Your mom—she just *gets* you."

It was what Chris had said. Donal nodded. "She does. Maybe I'm even starting to get her."

At noontime they checked Zap's clock against true noon and corrected their course slightly. They were barely under water again when Jes spoke up.

"I think I've got it. Not all of it—that will take months—but what happened to the people who built the islands."

Even Mrs. Clemens, who was steering at the time, looked around at her. Mrs. Clemens turned around again immediately but spoke up. "Please, tell us."

The others kept their eyes on Jes, and her face grew pink as she picked up the first sheet.

"The people of the deep began to have children who could live in both air and water, and these children longed to explore the land and gaze up at the stars. They built halls where sea and air met, so that families could remain one, and all rejoiced.

"Centuries turned, and those who lived in both air and water had children that could live only in air. These spread out upon the land, and as they went, they forgot, but still some came back to their ancestors.

"More centuries passed, and the people of the sea saw that no more children were being born who could live among the waves. Then, the people of the sea went back to their homes far beneath the water and remembered the old ways while any still lived. When the last were gone, those on the islands who could still swim below the waves sank the islands, and sea and air were no longer joined. Many ships searched for a time until history became legend and legend became myth. There is no more for them to find. We are gone. We are gone. We live on in those who watch the stars."

There was a long moment of startled silence. Finally, Donal spoke. "They became us."

Jes nodded. "The ancient Dorns and the ancient Keschel. The first two civilizations to have writing, who were rumored to have technology better than what came after, but never had gunpowder or steel—because you can't make those underwater."

There was a kind of mourning in knowing that your far distant ancestors had reached towards the stars and lost the sea. It gave some perspective to the mystery of a missing father, that everyone was missing ancestors they had never known existed. *And we have the sea again. Not quite the way they did, but close enough.*

"Everything we thought we knew is wrong," Jes added. She grinned. "This is going to be the biggest development in scientific knowledge since the discovery of steam!"

"Wait, is that a good thing?" Chris asked.

Amalia shrugged. "I'm betting we're going to end up with new ways to blow stuff up."

Chris pumped his fist in the air. "Count me in!"

By the time they got close to the island, Blot looked like he was longer than the skiff and about as big around as Donal's waist. He had also learned to say a new word—*fuhd*—and to understand the concept that some things were *fuhd*, and others were not.

"Just how big is he going to get?" Jes asked. "Was his father full grown?"

"I think his father was only mid-sized." Mrs. Clemens was piloting, so Donal searched in his pack a minute and pulled out a fist sized sculpture of a sea monster wrapped around a castle, a six-fingered person on its back.

"That thing is *huge*," Jes exclaimed. "Wait, this looks like your castle!"

Donal nodded. "I think it was carved to look like my castle. I think the tunnels underneath my castle into the water weren't accidental at all."

"The six-fingered people had sea monsters for pets?" Jes sounded shocked, as though that were stranger than defying gravity and using crystal for paper.

"Maybe," Donal agreed. "Or maybe as friends. Blot is only five days old, and he knows two words. We were a year before we could do that." Donal paused. "Actually, maybe we are the pets."

"Whichever it is, Captain, it's time to find the way in," Mrs. Clemens interjected. They were passing through the harbor, avoiding anchors and fishing lines, and Donal directed her to the cliff wall under the castle. "Come on, Blot!"

The tunnel was wider then the lava tubes under the volcano had been. There was plenty of room for Blot to zip ahead of them and back. Donal called encouragement to the baby sea monster as Mrs. Clemens brought them up to the water chamber. An air-filled tunnel to their right led up to the chamber they'd left from only a week before.

Ahead of them were a gathering of people— their parents, Uncle Kegan, Alex—and in front was Donal's mother, with a barrel of raw fish. When

Blot's dark blue head broke the surface beside the skiff, she just smiled and tossed a large fish into the air for him.

"Mom!" Donal rushed out of the skiff before the door had finished opening. "You will never believe what we found!"

She hugged him, hard, before tossing another fish to the happy sea monster. "I think, after this introduction, I will probably believe everything else. But the most important thing is that you found your way home."

They shared the discoveries after dinner.

Dinner time itself was an excited description of the sea monsters, the volcano, and their daring escapes. Donal thought that their parents took it all rather well, with only Jes's father, King Willem, looking like he was trying not to hyperventilate.

The show and tell portion of the evening was rather less sedate. While Blot alone had entranced Chris's dad into long discussions of cryptozoology and the opportunity to study the life cycle of sea monsters up close, everyone was amazed at what they'd brought home. When Jes read them her translation of the triple-language sheet, all of the parents went silent, and Jes's and Amalia's mothers cried.

"This is the cultural phenomenon of our lifetimes, and if you'd delayed another week, it wouldn't have ever been found," Amalia's mother said. "Not that the response is all going to be positive, but this is worth some controversy."

"Why wouldn't it be positive?" Jes demanded. "It's a treasure trove of knowledge!"

The adults looked at each other the way adults always did when they didn't know what to say. "Some people get very upset when their ideas about the world turn out to be wrong," Donal's mom said carefully.

"Like Dark Mathis, who wanted to be the winner so badly that he tried to hurt the people who'd only helped him," Chris pointed out. "Some people are idiots."

Mrs. Clemens nodded. "Some people are. Some of us get smarter over time."

The adults turned to look at her, and Donal cleared his throat. If anyone was going to accidentally reveal too much, it would be Chris, but if it were from guilt, his money was on Mrs. Clemens.

"Chris and Amalia and I haven't showed you what we brought back yet," he interjected. He motioned for Chris to go first with his more ordinary treasures, knowing that no one would be interested in jewels once Amalia brought out the gravity defying disc.

Chris's treasures took a good half hour to go through and were easily worth the ransom of a rather larger Kingdom than all of theirs put together. Donal was pretty sure that most parents wouldn't have immediately started talking about museums instead of money, but as Amalia had said—all their parents were cool.

Amalia's technological treasures almost broke Uncle Kegan, and they agreed that they'd give it a few weeks before calling in any other experts so that he could examine them first. Donal, going last, wondered for a moment why he'd picked the human things himself, the carvings and pictures that showed life among these long-gone ancestors. He loved technology as much as Uncle Kegan did, but when it came down to it, he'd chosen memories. *If I'd had to choose, I would have chosen Blot over every bit of the treasure we rescued.*

When they were done, it was too late for anyone to go home, even by airship. As the others went off to their rooms, Mom had blankets and pillows brought down to the water room where Blot waited. She joined him there and handed him a cup of tea as she sat down with her own, watching Blot snuggle up to him.

"I found something else out there," he said softly, stroking the sea monster's indigo neck. "I think I found who I want to be when I grow up."

His mother only looked at him, smiling and open. He smiled back.

"I want to be smart, like Uncle Kegan. I want to be caring, like you. And I want to be a good dad, whether that's just to Blot or whether I have kids of my own someday."

She opened her arms, and he leaned against her while Blot leaned against him. "You will be. I've known that since you left your lab behind to come rescue me and the others last Spring." She hugged him tightly. "Who we are isn't what we think, Donal. It's what we choose when there's no time to think it through. I'm proud of your choices."

There were lots of kinds of treasure. There had even been a small piece of treasure in Robert's last words to him—*Any man worth knowing would be proud to have you as a son.* This, though, these words, this moment, was the finest treasure he'd ever known.

Hope Erica Schultz writes science fiction and fantasy stories and novels for kids, teens, and adults. Her first novel, the YA post-apocalyptic *Last Road Home*, came out in 2015, and she was co-editor of the YA anthology *One Thousand Words for War*, in 2016. Her stories have appeared in multiple anthologies and magazines.